PERPETUA

PERPETUA

Olga Broumas

COPPER CANYON PRESS : PORT TOWNSEND

Thanks to the editors of the following publications, where many of these poems first appeared: *The American Poetry Review, The American Voice, Antaeus* ("The Masseuse"), *Bad Attitude, Caliban, Calyx, A Celebration for Stanley Kunitz on His 80th Birthday, Contemporary American Poetry from the University Presses, Deep Down, A Field Guide to Outdoor Erotica, 5 A.M., Herland, Living They Can't Explain: Poets Respond to AIDS, Open Places, Outlook, The Parnassus Review, Poetry East, Provincetown Arts, St. Mark's Poetry Project, Sojourner, The Sonora Review, The Texas Review,* and *Womantide*.

The author acknowledges special thanks
to Lauren Richmond and Bruce Deely.

The publication of this book was supported by a grant
from the National Endowment for the Arts.

Copper Canyon Press is in residence with Centrum
at Fort Worden State Park.

ISBN : 1-55659-025-3
Library of Congress Catalog Card Number : 89-61455
Copyright © 1989 by Olga Broumas

Copper Canyon Press
Post Office Box 271
Port Townsend
Washington 98368

Contents

I

II

III

Happy who has seen the most
Water in life.

I

Mercy

Out in the harbor breaths of smoke
are rising from the water, sea-smoke
some call it or breath of souls,

the air so cold the great salt mass
shivers and, underlit, unfurls the ghosts
transfigured in its fathoms, some

having died there, most aslant
the packed earth to this lassitude,
this liquid recollection

of god's eternal mood. All afternoon
my friend counts from her window
the swaths like larkspur in a field of land

as if she could absorb their emanations
and sorting through them find the one
so recent to my grief, which keeps,

she knows, my eyes turned from the beach.
She doesn't say this, only, have you seen
the sea-smoke on the water, a voice absorbed

by eyes and eyes by those
so close to home, so ready to resume
the lunge of a desire, rested and clear of debris

they leave, like waking angels rising
on a hint of wind, visible or unseen, a print,
a wrinkle on the water.

Evensong

The silvery leaf of insouciance lifts off the bay past dusk
and with it, like breath
or the barely visible exhaust
preceding nuclear explosion, dazzling,

the sand shifts deep below the house.
I feel its tremor in my ear, pillowed
on the futon on the floor,
and through it other tremors,

Soweto, Palestine, the lower
American continent whose beauty and bounty
enervate our ghetto-bound conscience.
I float on my freedom my sleepless nights.

The bay, underhem
of our planet, link to my natal beach, blue algeous pinafore
home to whale and fleet,
no longer rests me. On it, the spit

of the Arab touches me,
the venom of the dispossessed inoculates me,
the vomit and sweat of the detained, soaked
into earth and filtered through it,

tenderly meet the fine white sand
as if what remained of suffering to speak
were love. I am held
in the field of my freedom,

for which I exiled myself as soon as I could,
blind as though a corneal membrane,
which I coiled all my life behind to break,
let in only intensities of dark and light,

and freedom was light shattering
the mesmer of high noon in the Aegean.
Held there, my body weeps,
meets these marine broadcasts with a sadness,

dry, spasmodic,
elusive of CAT scans and sleeping pills.
By day, I ask of those who come to me for answers,
what would you say, asked by a poet

whose tongue and nails have been removed, whose nipples
are cratered with ash, to account for your freedom?
Seize it! I urge,
and return by night to my seizures. Peace and serenity

are the temple I shape, whose officiate,
joy, is choking.
Some may be seen beating her
on the back with clubs, others

with tubes down her nose enjoin her to vigor.
The beauty of strawberries,
organic and hand-picked by my neighbor,
in the blue bowl by the open window under circling gulls,

is likewise insufficient to rouse this Demeter from her bane.
Daily I make my offerings,
nightly receive the clash of the objectors,
those who squeeze tissue salts from humans for their brine.

Like a pit in the fruit's ripe stomach,
encircled by airborne toxins clouding its permeable skin,
I am nourished, gratefully,
by the force of an unconditional

habit still linking life to the pulp of fruit.
Gestures of offering, smooth forearms of receiving,
between them the vivid colors of rare untainted food,
like a brooch with its gem,

are the medals we're known by and carry, how long,
into disarmament, to joy's free breath again above our heads.

The Masseuse

Always an angel rises from the figure
naked and safe between my towels
as before taboo. It's why I close
my eyes. A smell
precedes him as the heart
fills from his bowl. I bow
down to the riddle of the ear,
its embryonic sworl nested with nodes
that calm the uncurled spine,
a maypole among organs.
Each day a stranger or almost
crosses my heart to die
from the unsayable
into the thickened beating
of those wings and we are shy.
Or frightened as with clothes
on we forget
abysmally what heaven
shares with death: what gypsy vowels
unshackled from the lips
rush the impenetrable
mind and the atlas
clicks in my trowel hands.
Crocuses on the threshold's south
side then and now. It goes on
like an egret scaling the unruly bands
of atmosphere we have agreed on
by my palms'
erratic longing of the flesh
to try. Toes crack. Hips
soften and the spine,
a seaweed in the shallow spume,

undulates like a musical
string by the struck note,
helpless with harmonics.
Rock. Cradle the perceptible
scar of the compass, sensible
stigma in a poised blind
of trust angling for reentry,
and the rain, the wind
across its face like minnows in the dark
of love schooling the light
will speak to you and you will walk
home dizzy, grazed by the gloaming and the just
illumined stars.

Stars in Your Name

All day you stare at us
who may not touch
your weeping or your blood.
HEATHER McHUGH

Kind, kind,
milk in the mind,
milk in the child,
child in the blind

hormone of sleep,
at night, supine,
anchored paralysand,
flat as a star

soaked in the hopeful calcium
all mammals
like a prayer paging god lie down
to weep out for our young, mild

soporific milk
endure our cry
issuing ineluctable
and somewhat like a bird

in flight out of an oil spill,
a black bird that had just been white,
a brother from the cratered tit,
aureoled, blue, perennial,

in orbit in the buckled sky,
o soul on its invisible

tether from the dippered
water that was self, now

rise through the historical
ocean-skin that divides
the dreaming anchor from its days, each night
a nipped rehearsal for the unrequited

vessel filling, filling in a child's
mind since the shock *unfair*
took it by force,
unfairly into concept,

and Justice, signal star,
tore from its center to abide
above the ferns and shelters
where in dreams a life

soars up to lick the fabled light
from its inverted triangles,
paired fairly in the sky,
glowing from our perspective

a phosphor that might nightly heal
the hole in the clay
flowerpot and brim
the unknown nourishment that balsamed,

angel with open eyes, untarred
and gleaming feathered lets
our solace be your
flight.

Mitosis

Resist anxiety
itself the making beautiful some abstract
you
in the continuing light
perennial water moving
its overwhelming percentage through
us its visible tide
unconnected and unified

to be alive

you said
time embraces
as we embrace behind the white
window-door meters from the bay
in our sideways fashion
and the exclamations
bright trumpetflowers behind us
in later memory
that evening say
you out I in
adorned

solitude and affection

rarely
even if everyday
the heart moves in its little
sideways thrust over gravity
to an exalted place composed of ringing
pitch so exact
inaudible it sweetens

the air whose luminosity
amber sweetens my lungs

memoryweed

burning at noon on the island hills
invoking a natural theater
where the arenas of possibility
are enlarged
in the speechless intense camaraderie
of instruments when their players
without ceasing their music

leave.

No Harm Shall Come

to my sister journeying toward
me with her piano
fingers capably
spread over her child
as she holds him
to herself in a front aisle
of an airplane over ocean.
She is leaning
neither forward nor back.
She is joking
with a steward
and she has taken off her shoes and feels her feet
larger since birth
spread on the fallen blanket a sensation
she enjoys
and turns to her window
like clouds.

Last week a friend of great intelligence
and compassionate beauty said she'd not feed a son
from her breast
because where
later find that enveloping orbit and why
introduce the need
I disagreed
but she would nurse a daughter
as she in turn could nurse
and something terribly awry
and black got twisted in my lungs.

Later talk turned to Sophie
                    and the incalculable guilt
                        of the survivor
            child chosen by a mother
under the extreme duress of the trainride
                    and the hissing name of the place
            chilling us still.
    To refuse the guilt is an act of life
                we said, at the time I thought Life.
        It was outside the restaurant.
            Snow was falling.

Eye of Heart

Because I was whipped as a child
frequently by a mother so bewildered
by her passion
her generous hunger she would freak
at the swell of her
even her love for me
alone in the small house
of our room by the Metropolis and fling me
the frantic flap of her hand as if some power
in me to say I want brought the unbearable
also to her lips

and as it didn't hurt
nearly as much as her distress
imagined it and set the set I grew up longing
for consummation as she did
beyond endurance
tenderness acceptance of the large
insatiable that grows so small
and grateful if allowed
its portion of sun

so that the images that led me down
the spiral of forgetting self and listing
like a phenomenon in the grip of its weather
dazzling or threatening but free
of civilization were the links
whereby her terror
made good its promise to annihilate
my will her will I couldn't tell
the difference then as now

when making love I can
breathe in forever on that rise
indefinite plateau whose briefness
like an eye is unselfconscious and the sphere
of the horizon its known line.

After Lunch

The PX wives who smuggled the dinette
set for my mother on Stadìou Street in 1956
sleep under their cilantro plants poolside in Arizona.
I sponge down the formica, lay the cloth and run
out to the car. It's not that far
but straight onto the mountain. It's a scar
among the dwarf pine scrub, bulldozers on each side,
the three-winged gate arching alone, a filigree of concrete,
the turned earth red, frank to the sky.
My pumps leave tractor imprints, it's the fashion,
snakeskin finesse and vibram sole. Here, she says,
a corner lot, a jaywalk from the chapel,
florist *en face*, a cosmic spot· she means
socially advantageous. Her best friend's over
there, by the far wall, terraced into abstraction.
They all admitted it, she says, I drew the choice
plot. Midday at rest
buzzes and ricochets. She shows me where
the flowerbeds will meet the promenade, her word,
and then, the wild oregano
fuming above the future
graves, we go.

Périsprit

In the hospital, in the impartial beauty of sunlight,
he tells us, *do not weep. I don't know if I can*

come back, but if I can it will be through your joy.
Historical earth too small already to contain our dead.

In four years I will lead my mother to find the priest
walking through the garden of graves. He is ready and she

does not walk with us behind the chapel where, unearthed,
an armful of bones in a tin ossuary bathed in red wine

is set in the sun and the long night through evening
to another dawn under stars to dry.

On Earth

When we drove up to the curb the woman
in the dun-colored house stained by the rain of days
when this was a village beyond the city
came to the gate to shrilly
claim the parking space.
She argued with my mother, unpacified
by the steady line of the wall
and the small rear entrance
we needed to reach
across the street, but my mother
mildened by it said "half an hour, half
an hour" and we crossed.
My uncle was there. I held my sister
and then her husband wheeled
his motorbike along the lane, helmet in hand.
We waited for the man
whose job it was to see the bones were ready.
Sometimes the flesh is slow.
Sometimes a daughter buries her mother
twice in the reddish earth as mother had.
All the allowable extensions
having passed we waited
holding a bottle of wine. The priest
came to take it saying
it was good, the bones
were dry. Uncle and I
followed him to the washing house:
a dun marble sink through the limed
doorway — by its step
two ossuaries stop our feet. The priest
directed my attention gently
from the smaller bones
I instantly chose as father, dapper, petite, lithe

dancer in uniform at Easter, leading his
circle of men, to the raw and bold
armful deeply stained
already by the wine. Earth, blood, vine.
We said a benediction. The widow
of the small-boned man held up his picture
and his ring. He had been bald and portly.
Through the heat,
the moisture rising from the sprinkled earth,
the crickets and the flies and bees, the distant
scrape of digging, the thin
voice of my sister rose
and rounded the chapel to meet me.
I held it so it too could see.
Good bones. Thick bones. Bones drinking deep.
I carried them,
with the woman whose job it is,
further behind the chapel
for their day in the sun and vaulted night
and wrote a number on the box in magic marker
I gave back to the woman with a tip.
My uncle was telling a detailed story
about his alarm clock and how it broke
and he returned it to the store and got a new one
thirteen months later with a new
guarantee. My mother, his sister,
listened to him. We walked to the front
gate to sign the papers
and back past the famous Sleeper
that drove its sculptor mad by never waking
to our car and the quiet
landswoman eating the noonday meal
with her husband, his truck pulled to the yard.

The Pealing

As in a parable the truant father
arrives. The birth
attendant there and I
distrust him but our panting

friend accepts him and we three begin
with her the three days broken
in portions of seven
agonizing breaths

and the uncounted minute
and a half we sleep
between them like a heart
rests calculable

lengths of lifetime
between beats.
Each third and fourth
breath brings her eyes to panic

so fierce her head tilts
on the axis
her eyes locked into mine
and once again I am

inside the camp
the peaked cap
and eyes implacable
and blue with pleasure.

Souls rose up with the smoke
and settled over Europe
as now the random hot
spots of Chernobyl.

Some say the hippies
now the Greens
are these souls born.
I recognized the Jewish toes

of Esther, the scholarship
girl from Athens in the pool
at the American consulate
cocktail party honoring the brain

drain we were part of
and bent to kiss them in the stupor
of that event before her
eyes held mine and we both

stopped. I live
since then with Jews.
I leave the room
where my Armenian

friend exhales
and sleeps for ninety seconds
and rouses and breathes and screams and sleeps
her third night

before dawn
to weep. So many
born. Such
natural pain

and still the clubs the whips
barbed wire cattle prods napalm
Klansmen and Afrikaners.
On break a midwife

talks me down. On Demerol
at last my friend is sleeping
deeper between pains.
I cross the hospital

to see another friend
and help him shift position
and suction his mouth and hold
his gaze. "White cars," he rasps,

"bridge sky." Twelve hours
to his death. Equinox.
March flowers
lunge in the heated air

petals omnivorous, pistils
throbbing. I make it back
by noon to tell him it's
a boy. The head spilled

blue, cyanic, ocean blue
in flat dawn light, pale blue
and sudden in six breaths and Beth
stopped a long moment

as in strobe
elbow to knee
inscribed dark totem with two heads
one fierce, one blue.

The obstetrician slipped the cord
loose from his neck
they howled
he flopped

rubbery and engorged.
Plum testicles:
waxy, veined, seamed
still to the tree.

Parity

This side of the post
apocalyptic treason I

pledge allegiance to the infant
raising its spine above the sand

of history to fit
its genitals to it to reach

from hand to mouth
the bitter sun-encrusted grains

it sprays back from its gums
mixed with its blood and spittle

on the adjacent sea
calming the spot of midday surf

time and again with glee as with
a seasoned fisherman's technique

of olive oil flung with sand to still
the trembling water.

Eros

On Death's face all religion dances
like pins on the head of a clit
and from that ground draws its defiance.
The nuclear menace can silence us

if we are atheists or lead us to think so
but here's Death, at least, behind our shoulder standing
as the not-without-which of the nightingale's
ability to thrill us past midnight

willingly on a south facing slope.
Atheists plead insomnia.
We reach past sunlight to its savor
midnight recreation of noon like helium lift

midbelly, luminous, melon-bright like its satellite
counterpart in some phase in the skies, in tune,
full face to its provider of heat.
Therapy, healing, the active

state of peace roots in summer, and harvest,
war's opposite, in heat begins its ontogeny.
In sex, the eye-slice of my head
dissolves as bay and sky infix

in the face of and because of what
we do not know, won't know, can't know
and would rather our eyes melt down
our face, our mass

irradiate in instant vapor,
our shadow implanted on the molten rock,
than know. We love
while oranges absorb their deadly ration,

the wheat is withdrawn from our markets,
the Pershings carry their sixty madmen
like clone Persephones half-lives beneath the sea,
madmen jogging the drab green

bays of the submerged bullet in drab green, a drab
meal microwave-silent in their gut, earphones
plugged to pillows, also green, on generous
coffin-sized shelves from which the meat

is long due recalled and most of them
just past eighteen. While the chickens
are bred without claws or beaks for easy packing,
the bluefish, striped bass and perch float up

cancerous, while the President
eats the last hormone-free meat,
while the Holland tunnel smells sweeter
than Paris in springtime and emission controls

are still being repealed,
while thank god the Dutch young
push their antidote for apartheid, only a word
like a song badly needed around which the lips

of the heart with their hunger can suck:
vrijheid, vrijheid
and the new Rainbow Warrior leaves their harbor
for the antipodes of defeat.

If I just have ten days I will fiddle.
One hundred years is as short.
Swell my strings, thump my drums, faith
like orgasm is problematic in the mind,

having no currency to bank. Its current
must be seized to be. When I'm risen, suddenly
past my brood of errands and their constant talk
like that of children a mother learns

out of love, part time, to ignore —
beer, bread, holy beard of an organ
that shrinks and grows psychedelic as Alice
in Steinian wonderland.

Even grammar sprouted tongues eager for that face.
Tender cows, holy buttons.
Gertrude the dervish in a field of words,
encoding the dogma: strategies

for prolonging pleasure are the faith
of oxygen fucking the lungs of life.
I believe the explicit is its own shield.
The godless see metaphors

while the born-again daily are
to dally among the miracles.
Why else be given astounding organs.
Why else given jungles where the improbable

not only grows rampant and awesome but provides
a good percentage of the globe's oxygen besides.
Amazon basin. The text
of sex, word for word and by heart

divined, enacted
in the antechamber of the soul so kindly
also provided me, is my guide and prayer.
When my skull shears and the sky

fills in I'm found.

The Massacre

I understand Xerxes' command to wield the whips
on the intractable, bereaving apron of the sea.
I beat the foam with racquet and with bat
hoping the tangled plant
in my therapist's office will escape
the havoc of my grief and when it thrives
from week to week increase
the fervor of my sickle
arm soughing the calm
air in her witness. A murderous
growl like a machete flattens
the delicate bronchi where the lungs
come to a stem. The ghosts are with us
poured from bruised tissue like the blood
I spray, embarrassed, on cream sheets. My scream
is tireless, my arm its pump. I hate the arrogant
poet who last night remarked
how much the natives recollect their wars
beside the birthplace of the ancient
memory he came to paste
onto his suitcase between Rome
and Istanbul, Berlin, New York, a gaggle of invaders
around the nameless, dusty, unmarked shore
young Homer roamed. Suitcase rhymes
with exile only for a native. I had to learn
it rhymes with the Bahamas for the touring clerks
who keep the books that feed on distant, ill-
remembered war. Two Germans walking home one dusk
cracked a boy's arm
across their thighbone like a faggot
and threw him on the pavement
writhing. It was fall. The fabled

light of Athens shone
on the protruding bone. Their boots
were new. They raised
the infected dust and in the silence
of the boy's disbelief and pride
the untold eons hide.

2

The friends of the dead lie on my table.
I do what I can
with their breath and my hands.
Witless, the birds are singing.
The crocus-garland month lengthens our light.
I want it
always to be light. I fight the night
and win. I peel my eye
against the black and white
T V until it dawns then sleep.
The Palestinian and Boston
homeless split the screen.
Number of children living on Brazilian streets.
What is forty million? Jeopardy's prey still the camera
their stripped and stunning faces
emblazoned in the halogen
a kind of sustained lightning
and the peasant heart
who counts the seconds between flash
and fall of thunder shrinks
from the looming toll.
Horror is toxic.
The lesions
on our organs keep the score.
The gentle and the hard are being taken
in legions and the globe
might shake us off its flank like quarry dust
and start again with something less
free, less
wrecked by greed but it suffers us
on its blue cetacean patience
like festered barnacles.

Like counted sheep midair over a stream
the friends of the dead pause on my table.
The shofar is ringing like starlight
too young to have reached us.
I do what I can
with their breath and my hands.

3

There were bombs in the womb, pulsing
the dark with adrenaline, stunning
the skinless swimmer, fusing
resistance to the bone.
The body of my mother
likewise was carried home
in pandemonium. An even score
of generations swam
through bootcamp to the shore
of first light, freed
to fight or flee
the random detonations
of Pasha or Nazi whim.
Only the land, the home
invaded, raped in, lit
like straw gave up
the rubble to rebuild.
The tongue
our tongues were pierced for speaking
moonlight bright, shine all night
help me learn to read and write
rose from the fertile
ash. Whole men
were roasted on the spit.
The gatherers of children
roped them in.
Women would rather jump
in the ravine than breed
the bastard offal.
Rinsed hair and aprons
dripped a serpent
path from well to rim.

I understand the urge
to beat and maim and kill.
If I were Black,
which I am,
if I were Jew,
which I am,
Irish, Palestinian,
native or half-breed,
which I am, I am
homeless or disappeared,
immigrant or queer —
Resinous weeds
grow taller where the water
fell on the craggy slant.
I pound the mattress.
What I don't understand
holds us back.

The Moon of Mind
Against the Wooden Louver

The visitors in room 8509
stand in a circle chanting something Russian.
The Hassids down the hall have come
in segregated silence, men
roll their thick white stockings in the lounge,
mother and sisters still
between the door and bed each time I pass.
We step across invisible or merely transparent
shadows making up their mind
to speak, to intervene, to cull.

A firm hand – like the A.M. nurse sponging the last
few hours of confusion
from the somehow childlike
emaciated limbs and face she lifts,
a bride, I swear, swathed in a sheet,
back on fresh linen and then clips
the bottoms of the flowers
keeping the family at bay while Barry naps
in her unbridled trust – we lack.
Not without prayer. Not without

the pluck and humor of the song
your bones thrum while the blood still laves
their broadside and their flank.
I kiss your bones. In mind
each rounded pinnacle
of rib is white
against an O'Keeffe sky and light

their lingua franca. Such thinking heals
the moment. It divides us
for its duration like a cyclone

fence from our despair, our rage, our bitter greedy fear.

Touched

Cold
December nights I'd go
and lie down in the shallows
and breathe the brackish tide till light

broke me from dream. Days I kept busy
with fractured angels' client masquerades.
One had a tumor
recently removed, the scar

a zipper down his skull, his neck
a corset laced with suture.
I held, and did my tricks, two
palms, ten fingers, each a mouth

suctioning off the untold harm
parsed with the body's violent grief
at being cut. Later a woman
whose teenage children passed on in a crash

let me massage her deathmask
belly till the stretch
marks gleamed again, pearls
on a blushing rise. A nurse of women HIV

positives in the City
came, her strong young body filled
my hands. Fear grips her only
late at night, at home, her job

a risk on T V. It was calm, my palm
on her belly and her heart
said Breathe. I did. Her smile
could feed. Nights I'd go down

again and lie down on the gritty
shale and breathe the earth's salt
tears till the sun
stole me from sleep and when you

died I didn't
weep nor dream but knew you
like a god breathe in
each healing we begin.

Walk on the Water

Chafed ocean, a chadored moon
fluting the supple acres,
the silver spine of surf drawn from

a shore still resonant, each sounding
molecule discrete yet filled
with sameness so continuous

we might believe you too
though drawn from us instill
us who are left

with eucalyptus resin on our fingers,
after the flowers,
torn from styromoss,

have drowned the hollow grave, its sound
of metal against bone, although
the earth was rained on, soft

the hands on the shovel as if one last time
your arm – peace
is that continuity,

you were trying to tell us,

faithful and loyal to the last
you were cast from, friend
in the vibrant elements,

song without skin to hold.

Before the Elegy

FOR PAUL

Midbay, the Nikonos,
a pun on the bright island
of my childhood, sinks
its waterproof housing
guided by hand not eye,
to the burly and the slight
blond figures casting through
the wide brimmed net
of light against the bobbing boat.
The frightened photographer is brave.
Shut tight, her eyes
relinquish to the skin their grasp.
They surface, all three
explosions of lung made light
and drop again to fly
arms wide
two dancers and a feeling eye
into the dolphin-liquid dark
that holds them as a bird in sky.
More, more than we believe
gives light.
The hair, the beard, the nimbus
on the glans, the sheath
around the plummeting,
the seaweed and small fish
are stars against the lapis night.
Stretched out
across the screen the slides
force us like ocean to hold breath

on land. We hold,
the slight-built German and his wife,
the large blond man who rowed the boat,
the artist and her girl and I,
illumined by the tangible
dream of the flesh made kite.

Native

Driving with mother to the shore,
northwest then south from Athens,
deep black and straw-gold earth
arched with the white ejaculate
the mobile force of irrigation,
to a mountain pass,
as through a mouth,
iron-red cliffs above
my father's village.

Olivegrove, poplar, silverleafed
the stark descent,
as if his soul had pared
the way through these
benefic mountains,
ridges receding in a haze
of heat over the omphalos
at Delphi.

Adelphae, siblings I and she
in the irradiated steam
of thyme around that belly.

Rust earth, mauve sea,
zigzag at zero altitude at dusk,
mesh-aproned hills and bell-flocked sheep,
home stretch.

So much of that
acreage and livestock was to burn
in August's tilt from rain,
watering wheels in charred fields without hoses.

We bathed in the sea
by the house they built,
two weeks unsnarling the garden,
dahlia from bougainvillea,
arguing only how much salt
to eat at last.

After *The Little Mariner*

I woke up in the dark
of a moon steamed against glass
black as if glazed with ebony
or soft lead handled in the blind
of another's dream and he
the crossroader
the atmospheric horseman
the marksman who can calm the deep
by taking a teenager

down from his constellation and instructing
him to walk across the surf then kneel
inside the pelago a broadcast
charging the elements
with Rilke's terror as my soul
rang in the air above
the bedclothes rustled though my limbs
on the bed were paralyzed
transparent

I could see
a ribbon song begin
from the lungs of his penis
inside my body like a swallow
of ice-cold milk in August
gleaming and slow like mercury
upstream and through my lips
and then my soul
fell into or my body rose.

II

Amberose Triste

Beautiful sex whose lips I know
hasten to light and deep to darkness

shaven from your lair
where

in the lateral maternal
blue by California

chill now
your amber drink and smoke.

Lengthen in repose
as the evening on its way

from me is apersonal
your matutinal

leap into dawnstruck light
from the sated Atlantic

a planetary motif.
Salt through the earth conduct the sea

skull, patient surface.

After

Words are black where there are stars.
I'll never have a child you said this morning.
I can't remember when I made up my mind.
Mind, child, stone. The heat
flattens and coats them. They turn
from black to white and whiter, air. The wind
blows them back into place again and the grass
heaves a little where they had lain.

Next to the *Cafe Chaos*

the lambent cobblestones refract the blue
and yellow of *L'Afreak Electronique*
into a frazzled dayglow
batting the piss-crossed wall that jogs
the curved canal from *Milky Way*
to ambient *Paradiso*
regulars spiking the street.

Under that blinking sign,
the neon-pale geraniums rappelling
on burgher curtains drilled with light
at night and night
tobacco-stained by day, we lunge
made slow by the urge to love
untrammeled by the sirens'
aggrandizing thrust. A gaseous flame

leapt from the greengold filth of the canal,
the squatters' barricades lit up and their anointed faces
appeared in the journalistic probe
outlined in kohl like convict masks.
Unhinged from the mirage

and refuged on a park bench by the swan's
imperial sashay we splay
a fist across each other's back
and loaded with fact like methedrine
by the unvanquished halo from the *Terra
Incognita's* strobe we hug.

To Draw the Warmth of Flesh
From Subtle Graphite

The architecture gives more comfort than the scenes
enacted in its armature, cream-quilted beds
divided by the skylight into squares
of sun and shade like alternate sensations
abandoned as by picnickers on shore.
How light the paper is

on which this all is drawn,
the ladder of old olive by the tub,
a recent innovation, buckles it with its gnarls.
The terrace door above sheds bars
of summer shadow through the rungs
and tiles the floor with diamonds.

We aren't there to mar the lazy arc
of light along its path from wall to trapdoor.
On the beach, where we might be, it's calm,
and also by the olive groves and asters.
The terra cotta tiles absorb the sun.
The village bell layers the air, birds, then an airplane

fly a line into the distant sea. The language
of the people there amid the smells
announcing dinner rises.

The Eye

Ftu, ftu, spit on her when you say that . . .
She'd pounce upon the evil eye, its magnitude
reflected in an oil drop's spread
on water, and those teeth. She'd loosen
and push them out her mouth at me to keep
me still. Then, if I was sickly, vulnerable
to compliment, the fork's black tines,
cotton-wrapped, were dipped
in alcohol a cool and tangy blue, lit,
thrust into kitchen glasses that in turn
were quickly applied to my chest and back,
so that the starving oxygen sucked blood
from my congested lungs into the vivid
mounds of flesh inside the rim.

Its lip came off with a hearty thwack
and gave its name to a kind of kiss,
vendouza. Mother repeated her routine,
and later I taught it to my lovers as it lifts
desire's envy from its burden on my clavicle. Still,
I'd had a viral exanthema of the throat for weeks.
My car was totalled while parked.
The sulfa caused lesions from B deficiency
and doctor said herpes. The druggist
wrote four × daily instead of twice.
I worked my two jobs and slept. Weeks.
I was polite to the eye,
like someone who suppressed the will to injure,
transparent and deflecting, but no avail.

One night, I filled a bucket with bay water
and trailed circles of salt around the house.
They would return, I intended it,

whatever it was to its source and *afflict affect* it.
It sounded Turkish. I was determined and I observed myself,
not surprised but for the first time.
The exanthema lingered but I was alert
and returned to the dilation
of non-verbal occupation and hours alone.
As I do not believe in a personal god,
nor in personal energy on the biofield level,
I was momentarily unconfirmed on hearing the flautist
I'd loved and been avoiding had poured
cleaning solution in her contact lens and stung her eye.

I called her, because there is
no personal energy on the biofield level,
though the imagination joins stars and names constellations
and god is posited and really lifts us thereby.
Seam of the Universe, she said, remember?
Yes, good luck, I said.

Between Two Seas

Tonight I think of Bouboulina,
the poetry she used against the Turks
to code intelligence in rhythm
from mountain to ravine to creek
and the subservient-looking peasants who worked there.
Only as strong as who came before us sings a tape

I use while working on my clients,
and I don't have the heart to edit it
though I dislike lyrics during bodywork
as too much enlisting the conditioned
mind in a direct communication between fields.
As I approach middle-age, with the thrill,

more than unexpected, astonishing,
of having reached a mountain peak
after a decade's dawdling, accustomed so
to hoisting the self the stress
seems natural, and lifting
my eyes over the edge

in the resigned manner ascribed to maturity,
prepared to see the pinnacle then eke
another forty, human nature permit, inclined
downhill, only to stand before a broad
horizon-reaching mesa, full of brooks (in C Major
for viola d'amore, the Greek

poet said), hills, valleys, blooms and all
the accoutrements of fauna a pastoral
metaphor can hold, an era broad, stable

and, in its upright stance, humane.
Endurance, serenity brought through
the blasphemous contradictions of an adolescence

to mid-thirty (until I lost all trace
of girlhood from my face, a friend said) clear
from heart to mind a threshing ground
where compassion, outrage, dignity
share breadth the sexual alone
had augured with its olive branch

let loose each time to fly.

She Loves

deep prolonged entry with the strong pink cock,
the situps it evokes from her, arms fast
on the climbing invisible rope to the sky,
clasping and unclasping the cosmic lorus.

Inside, the long breaths of lung and cunt
swell the vocal cords and a rasp a song,
loud sudden overdrive into disintegrate,
spinal melt, video hologram in the belly.

Her tits are luminous and sway to the rhythm
and I grab them and exaggerate their orbs.
Shoulders above like loaves of heaven,
nutmeg-flecked, exuding light like violet diodes

closing circuit where the wall, its fuse box,
so stolidly stood. No room for fantasy.
We watch ourselves transform the past
with such disinterested fascination,

the only attitude that does not stall
the song by an outburst of consciousness
and still lets consciousness, loved and incurable
voyeur, peek in. I tap. I slap. I knee, thump, bellyroll.

Her song is hoarse and is taking me,
incoherent familiar path to that self we are all
cortical cells of. Every o in her body
beelines for her throat, locked on

a rising ski-lift up the mountain, no
grass, no mountaintop, no snow.
White belly folding, muscular as milk.
Pas de deux, pas de chat, spotlight

on the key of G, clef du roman, tour de force letting,
like the sunlight lets a sleeve worn against wind, go.

With God

In another life in a convent I
attending the aphrodyte
by constant dilation and distillation
of devotees
visitors or communicants
delighted alike
upslope the inverted bowl of the polis
where the omphalos spasm was felt to exist
a fault and throttle at the hearth
central to the foundation.

It pleased us
and god too to extract
from each adoration many
successive radiations
toward the sweet god bathing
in the eternal basin below
by our attention.

If I had said extract I'd have been tickled
and hot towels placed on my godly parts
funny rules
            I sweated it out
like waiting
for a smell to occur
as in early March
in the hardy bud
of the lavender fields
of our region.

No drawing back for fear of drawing
such pleasure away. Athletic.

Etymology

I understand her well because I too practice love
for a living. She came for therapy which I explained
from the root *create,* as in the cognate *poem,*
and *theros,* summer harvest and heat,
and how the ancient prostitutes, *therapaenidae,*
practiced the poetry of heat. She had
enjoyed the whoring but not the pimp
she railed against
so loud in our fourth session
I ducked to keep the pressure with my thumbs
and covered my ears with her breasts to bear her decibels.
"Red trails of poison up my thighs, goddamn him.
Beat on my head all day last time I saw him,
and when the cops arrived, *Her boyfriend*
beat her up. Stopped by to see if I could help.
He had the bad luck later to blow a cop.
Tooth and heart. Isn't everything?"
No. Faith as prelude and spine.
That is a more important.
That is a larger that.

Tryst

The human cunt, like the eye, dilates
with pleasure. And all by joy never named

now are priceless in the magnitude of the stars.
From are to are, have to have, beat sub-eternal.

By day, I found these on the beach, for you each
day and give. By night, remind me, I have

forgotten. Action replied by action, peace by peace.
Take you in all light and lull you on a sea

of flowers whose petals have mouths, mesmerized
centerfold, upsweep toward sleep.

For Every Heart

I like it when my friend has lovers, their happy moans,
unrestrained, fill the house with the glee of her prowess.
As in China, during the concert of the laser harp,
cameras added their applause, percussive,
while the umbilical fanned neon from each note
in the open-air theater and ribboned the path of·stars,
I am moved to clap. Hands clapping calm us.
It is their simple, wholehearted and naive sexual imitation
their fleshbird dance chest-high in the open of time.

Field

I had a lover. Let us say we were married, owned
a house, shared a car. The trees were larch, white birch,
maple, poplar and pine, the mountains granite,
and three months of the year verdantly lush. We met

cows, sheep and horses on our walks up or downhill
a fine dirt road. In time, my lover came to take
another lover, of whom I also became enamored.
There is a seagull floating backward in a rare

snowstorm on an Atlantic Ocean bay as I remember this,
its head at an angle that suggests amusement.
This younger lover flew home to a far southern state
and returned in a large car with several rare instruments

and a Great Dane, a very spirited animal who had to
be returned to a family estate in the Midwest soon thereafter,
having discovered and devoured a neighboring farmer's chickens.
The seagull flies laboriously into the wind

the length of my windows, then settles to be floated back.
It is a young bird, wings black-tipped and grey.
We added a room to the cabin that summer, the work done
by a young sculptor from the college, one who seemed

to be continuously counting, a devotional attitude
that appealed to me. One evening we returned to find
a note pinned to our door, Call Ted abt a possible free piano.
That it did not materialize did not affect my feelings

toward him and in September I moved my area into this room.
Fifteen by seventeen, it had a long wall of salvaged windows,
a door with a sturdy ladder to the forest floor,
a wall of the enormous cedar logs of the main cabin

and, to it, a soundproof door with a double window
Ted had devised. Our younger lover took over my old area,
and my lover continued working upstairs
where the rising heat of the Franklin caused her

to take off her clothes frequently, as well as open a window.
We bought a large futon for my room, and next to it
laid a smaller futon, what is called a yoga mat, turned
the quilts sideways and slept facing the luminous birches

in differing night lights. Enormous fireflies
when the temperature hovers at thirty near midnight,
early September, late June. Daylight was often a wrathful time,
and it is a tribute to the height of our spirits

that we barely noticed, gliding over it as we did
over friends and professions. The phenomenon of three hearts
dilating as if in unison, eyes diverging toward
each one, rare, blasted our systems with tremendous energy

and within the year we packed each a bag, compromised
on five instruments, of which two collapsible, and a small amp,
and flew to a continent where one of us knew one country's
language. We traveled, fought, separated and reunited

for six months, then were joined by an old friend, traveling
with whom we thought a lover, who turned out
a companion instead, a tall, stately model with the gait,
approaching us on the beach, of a sulky seven-year-old.

Our younger lover's age, they played music together,
and together got stranded in an inflatable boat
whose outboard motor they'd flooded. *I sacrifice
myself to the sea,* chants our lover, unforgettable

in this scene if unwitnessed, as the model struggles
with the four flimsy oars and, *Row, damn it!*
They made it to shore half a mile east of our house,
and were towed by a small speedboat belonging to a man

who had tried to fix their motor, he standing in
his fiberglass, they trailing behind, past the entire
village on their wooden chairs outside the grocery,
the eating house, the front garden doors. The model

was extremely cheerful at dinner, having hauled the canvas
tub to the yard, our lover wounded in pride and spiteful.
We lived in that house on the edge of the water
for two months, until our money ran out and we returned

to our wooded hill, our friend and companion to their town
by the eastern tip of a Finger Lake, seven hours by car
further inland. My lover and I found our jobs
during our leave had been embittered by our firm's

acquisition by a larger establishment affiliated with
the military. We resigned, or rather, refused the new
firm's offer, and shortly thereafter moved to my friend's
town where I accepted a federally funded position for

my skills in music and massage, a divergence
that delighted me. We rented a farm out of town, partly
on work exchange, feeding and caring for two horses,
two dogs, one of them slightly mad, six cats and a senile

bunny. This our lover agreed to do, as well as stacking
most of nine cords in a fit of jealousy every morning
of the week my lover was in California. They were actually
face cords, the pile would have measured four and a half

in our old county. They made a terrific racket,
hurled across the yard into the barn, where the dogs
from their pen greeted them. The farm was on a straight
north-south road, they couldn't be trusted loose

in the four-wheel-drive traffic, they were barn animals
and couldn't be kept in the house, but their barking
from their large, humane, indoor-out pen with running brook
and bales of hay had an ungrateful sound that made us

ignore the fence when they broke it, to the chagrin
and later vituperation of the owner who kept our deposit.
My lover returned from California with three bottles
of fine red, one of them a Petite Sirah, purple velour

tops for us, and the seedling of a new self profoundly
and coincidentally engendered by a brief affair with
the lover I'd left to move East to our cabin. Our younger
lover didn't recognize the smell under the fingernails

as I did, with pleasure. It is impossible to disengage
from jealousy someone told me in graduate school.
It challenged me to find a course that wouldn't feed it,
and have put my mind to it since, profiting only

from a general graciousness, nonchalance, fatality. The snowfall
that winter was heavy and the winds tore savagely to one side
of our four-mile road. By what should have been midspring
our lover had contrived to be collected to the faraway

southern state and we did not care to pursue the deposit.
Though we were broke, a sensation like shutters beating
bodily in the stillness that followed the April storms
preoccupied us exclusively, though I did see the lilacs

crashing it seemed through the old barn walls,
and the hill go green on the stain of the bellyshot doe
before the snow. We moved, with my friend, to California
for a summer job arranged by my old lover, and we four

spent the season specifically amiably, in fairly rigid
pair formation, I and my friend — who had first become
my lover under my younger lover's hand while abroad by the sea,
a gesture delicate and precise, savored by all and regretted

bitterly and immediately by the youngest — my old lover and
my lover. We lived and worked, teaching nutrition, healing
and survival skills to young adults, in what had been a Navy
compound on a Pacific coast beach and had long hours

of simple sitting, and staring. I brought my guitar
and practiced hearing in detail my picking against foghorns
and gulls. My lover sang. My friend was a little insecure
far from home, and clung, peacefully, to my middle.

In the fall we moved to be half the staff at the halfway
house here. The pay was low but secure and we each rented
a studio facing the bay for the off season. We did not travel
together. Rather, my lover flew directly, my old lover

via the Midwest to visit family, and my friend and I
drove the car. *Snow Creek, Lake Crescent, Ruby Beach,
Humptulips, Tokeland, Palix, Parpala, Hug Point, Arch
Cape, Perpetua, Darlingtonia, Bliss 14, Pacific Fruit*

*Express, Grace, Power County, Sweetwater, Harmony,
Adora, Amana, Homewood, Vermillion, Presque Isle.*
We've lived here four months, a full holiday season,
friends from inland and the West. My lover and I

bicycle the dune roads to the ocean. The winter is mild,
and the bay home to seven varieties of duck that I've
sighted, and seagulls and pipers and pigeons that sit
on the railing to hear the guitar and are annoyed

and shift and scold if I should lose my concentration
for their flattery. My friend and I cook meals for our
festivities, and make love for exquisite hours when I may
scream and contort myself but on leaving the house

remember nothing, no, not nothing exactly, I remember
if put to it, but not ordinarily. My old lover and I
are affectionate, my lover and I are cheery, and our
younger lover recovered and moved to a large city nearby

and infrequently visits my lover and lately, lightly, me.

Lying in

Morning.
Who never sang before is singing.

That open avenue, tree-limned,
by which is known a city
domed palatino to triumphant arch,
that fountained thoroughfare,
banked by the broad facades, bone-white,
of arcade shade in sun,
that splendid rectilinear
lay of center city, not wholly
squared but bowed as was
known to the Greeks, physical
marble memory of sheaved-
in-a-column trees, eternal
iconostasis whose noon
is twelve and midnight six o'clock,
hill-cradled basin
transfigured as by tiers
of balconies where linens
gently take the air
between their seams and pull
against the balustrades
to join the light, that
swath, that aqueduct become,
like the cherubim and seraphim
we must aspire to, nothing
but eye, view, opening
to light, that fairway
whose incarnations recollect
god unknown
and immanent as faith
feeding on our emotions,

that crown, that head
bone having moved
to the hilarious
wind of seed and blood
in sinuous symmetrical
rotation down the apse,
the apex of the body,
stairwell, *allea,* boulevard,
its split reveals
like Bashō's fish
the Buddha we have eaten.

The Way a Child Might Believe

I think now how we biked toward the sand
all day and up the hill at Devil's Elbow
in time to see a green ray, magma of the sun,
darken the dazzled rim of the Pacific.

We liked to feel the earth under our feet
turning as though our pedals made a difference,
as though it turned from Florence to Eugene
to kiss our wheels as we rode west to meet it,

sweaty and blissed. A borrowed bike at twenty-one
was like a Guggenheim. It rained. We laughed.
The sixty miles of woods have left a sound,
an imprint I return to in your image,

the way a childhood talismanic word
repeated will repeat the walls it echoed.
There are no walls. The day is green.
Green is the night, midfield on our returning,

cowed by the rain, asleep in our tube of tarp.
There is no who I was before that happened,
placeless and innocent, filled only
by a desire to have seen, have had

the carpet of stars infixed. As with your face.

Attitude

I let them whip and fuck me
engaged in a passion I did not want them

to understand. They used a paddle and their hands
were large, their cocks youthful and pretty,

one red and shiny and very hot, one blithely
sheathed. They played about me, tying, untying,

vying the better posture or hold. After supper
they rubbed my clit and made me count backward

from a thousand perfectly, fingerfucking my ass
before they'd let me come. Bright windy afternoons

mid-spring and early summer, tiger balm on the clit
to keep it hot. We were strangers in town and,

as we were leaving soon, felt free to bring
others home from the bar to fuck me, showing off

how they sucked my nipples from the side
to make me tremble and wet. I never touched them,

and they would tickle and lick each other
in camaraderie or greed, impatient for their turn.

We went to the movies on other nights.

Days of Argument and Blossom

Energetic and long,
the way a dolphin's swim tickles the sea,
you play with me, both right and wrong, and softly

the turning fern fans your ass.
I used to rub myself with sand,
nostalgic for salty idiom. Offer me

the nude world of your back. The wind
overturns a glass of water. Or, you turn.
Your palm, your suntanned breast, the triangle

of your elbow.
Earth on a new eve, no lover,
no later that won't echo as refrain

our forty-five seconds out of orbit,
end of May among wind-twisted pine,
the roof and terrace tiles

a crimson game of solitaire
against the saffron shadowbox of moon,
the species a score for chord instrument,

daylight and eye, and the eye
not apologizing, knowing
its scope beyond the periphery

of night cast on the physical
world from its stained
glass membrane, the apex

of its dome. What *if* one memorized
the *Iliad* in school? Stubborn and generous
about our pleasure let us be as we,

unaccountably happy here,
escape the wait to hear the spit
fall on the scythe of hours.

III

and for Susan

LUMENS

There are no secrets
It's just we thought that they said dead
When they said bread

JOHN CAGE

OH LORD

I love when you take over
Her eyes and pierce me with your sky

THE KNIFE

Love of life
I promise to remember you

Each time we meet is the last

Sex is the alibi

Tethered and bound
Our backs across the room
From each other we sing

THE BIRD

To make poetry's possible
At home even briefly in the human wild

EACH LOVE

Parallel
Infinite
Unequal

NIRVANA STAIR

I come from small seas littered with
Playful islands

Feel how my heart is shaped
By that sheltering

When you touched me
taking all that time
an ancient
and consecrated city
in orbit for centuries
found its dome

She has a big warm
          face and I love to
take it in my hands
          and smooth the cheeks out
with my thumbs
          The truth makes me excited
I fill you with it
          baby she says

Everywhere the cries of the tortured
I root my heels into the earth
my native health
and joy a mindless miracle

TATTOO

A child is a lonely thing to put in prison
Without a lover lonely in its parent's care

BRIDGE

A song unhinges bitterness easy enough from sorrow
Some vowel litany with stops to pass until
The most ordinary is not

To build the chair
To build the chair
To build the chair
To sit
To sit
Witness the mystery
World

PRIVACY

Finally
   the only one I want
     to caress is you

You watch the changing
   light across the sky
     I watch your eyes

TEACUP

Flared at the lip like clematis
One swallow
Raised bottom where the sugar sleeps

FLORIDIAN

It's not just that you're wet but that you're swollen
Ocean where for me you dip

Where desert boulders cleave: two stars
Small in the V, large up above

Where last I slept with you the tide
Eases the mark

DEVOTEE

I am grooming the body and rays of the sun
That will rise on the day you return

DETAIL

The mother's hand
In the latex glove
Approaching the lesion

The son's inconsolable
Weeping at the rubber
Bird he believes
Has died

SPEECH

Torturers
Breathing our human air
Full of our sounds like ornaments
Of an archaic language
Tender fair gift rejoice feed

THE DISTANCE

You were sitting by the green canal
Like the French in a rented chair
Whose curved iron back allowed your bare
Pale shoulders to be seen

And though you didn't speak
Or look at me you let me stand
Behind you for an hour
Touching them as the water flowed

To and from our eyes

THE RETURN

As when setting a candle
In the molten wax of the one burnt low
In the hot candelabra

Baby, I call you, you
In me as if

INTERVAL

Two months since I sucked your nipple first
Eggplant purple then fig blue the taste
Drawn from your inner body lingers

CHASTE

Asleep
Mouth to mouth
For an hour

DECOLLETAGE

You say it's lime but I say smoke
Quartz was squeezed for your perfume

Leave me the snake
It is the you before the screen while you are gone

SELFISH

It's true musicians please
The public with their pleasure, but we
Eschew the stage

THE VEIL

Chamois from your workbench
Brushed by your perfume
Prayer-rug incense rosary
And pillow in my pocket

NIGHT AND LIGHT

Because your hand is my hand and my eye
And taste and smell and spirit I am I

THE PEACEFUL FIST

I said inside the small
Cathedral of my cunt eleven years before
That awning
Rose round the folded altar of your palm

PERPETUA

As the seed of a mole for
Generations carried across
Time on a woman's belly
Flowers one morning blackly
Exposed to poison and poison
Itself is not
Disease but mutation is one
Understanding the strong
Shaft of your clitoris I kiss
As the exposed tip of your
Heart is another

Notes

NO HARM SHALL COME : *page 21*

Sophie : Sophie's Choice, novel by William Styron and film starring Meryl
Streep based on the Nazi practice of asking a mother, newly ar-
rived at a camp, to choose one among her children to accompany
her, while the others were shot.

AFTER LUNCH : *page 25*

PX wives : Wives of American military and diplomatic personnel abroad
who are entitled to shop at Post Exchange (PX) stores stocked
with American goods. My mother worked as a clerk in the Athens
store for several years, to secure the cost of my eye operation, but
was not allowed to make purchases.

PÉRISPRIT and ON EARTH : *pages 26 & 27*

Because Greece is so small and has been so densely populated over many
centuries, there is not enough cemetery space, especially in the
cities. This has given rise to the practice of burying the dead for
4–5 years, until only the bones remain, then excavating the bones
and placing them in small metal lockers stored in mausoleums.
Rarely, on unearthing, the melting, as it is called, is not complete,
and the remains must be reburied for a time. Though I was ex-
tremely agitated and apprehensive about witnessing my father's ex-
humation, the actual experience was one of relief and joy to have
him back on earth and in light with us again.

Dancer . . . leading his circle of men : My father was an officer of the Greek
army and on national holidays, dressed in a *tsolias* uniform of white,
thickly pleated kilt, red tufted shoes, red fitted jacket with medals
and braid, red fez and sword, led his command in the circular
dances of our people. While the rest of the dancers perform sober,
rhythmic steps, the leader, supported by the second dancer, leaps
and twirls, striking his heels and forehead in the air, and the
ground upon his brief return.

PARITY : *page 33*
Olive oil flung with sand : Technique used for shallow-water-fishing at
night. A rowboat is pulled gently through the water while a strong
light shines from the prow to illumine octopi and squid. Handfuls
of sand moistened with olive oil are flung as the boat advances,
which clarifies the water and improves visibility and aim.

EROS : *page 34*
Vrijheid : Dutch word signifying freedom and love, antonym of apart-
heid.

THE MASSACRE : *pages 38–43*
Xerxes : Persian king of the late fifth century B.C. who, unable to cross
the Bosporus on his way to war with Greece because of high seas,
ordered his men to whip the waters. This act was always presented
to us in school as ridiculous, though I see now that perhaps it al-
lowed his army to vent its frustration and persevere.

The couplet *moonlight bright. . . read and write* is a free adaptation of the
song Greek children would sing while walking at night to secret
schools in churches or cemeteries during the Ottoman occupation
of Greece from the 13th Century to the mid 1800s. The teaching,
and at times the speaking, of Greek was forbidden.

The gatherers of children : The Turks would routinely round up young
male children from the villages and raise them in elite military
camps. These young men, who then fought against Greek in-
surgence, were known as *yenitsari.*

Women would rather jump : This phenomenon was common enough to
generate its own dance in several regions.

I am indebted, once again, to Charles Wright for the poem's motif "If I
were. . . , which I am, if I were. . . , which I am," which has
stayed in me for nearly twenty years.

AFTER THE LITTLE MARINER : *page 51*
I had this dream the night I completed the last draft of the translation of
Odysseas Elytis' book of poems, *The Little Mariner.*

THE EYE : *page 61*

A common practice to ward off the evil eye is to spit disdainfully after paying a compliment, especially to a young or vulnerable person. Belief in the evil eye is very strong, and it is said that even a mother can lay the evil eye on her child through her admiration. Amulets are worn, or blue stones, to guard against this. When an evil eye does take, evidenced by inexplicable malaise or misfortune, spells are cast to remove it. They range from the mild, in which the practitioner's piercing gaze rests briefly on the sufferer's eyes, nose, ears, mouth, anus and urethra/vagina, while a drop or two of oil shook in a bowl of water embodies the evil drawn, to priestly exorcisms of varying complexity. The ritual with the flaming fork and kitchen glasses is known as cupping, familiar to acupuncturists, and is applied for decongestive and tonic purposes.

BETWEEN TWO SEAS : *page 63*

Bouboulina : Young woman from Peloponesos, instrumental in the successful revolt against the Turkish occupation of Greece. As an adolescent I lived on a street in Athens bearing her name, behind the National Museum.

SHE LOVES : *page 65*

Lorus : Umbilical cord

ETYMOLOGY : *page 68*

Therapy breaks down etymologically into *theros:* summer/harvest and *poio:* create. The Greek word for poet is synonymous with creator, as in the Greek Orthodox credo: I believe in one God, father almighty, poet of sky and earth . . .

FOR EVERY HEART : *page 70*

Concert of the laser harp : Concert given in China by Andreas Vollenweider on a harp whose each string released differently colored laser beams into the night when struck. On live recordings you can hear the clicking of cameras, like night insects, all through the performance.

LYING IN : *page 78*

Sheaved-in-a-column trees : It is theorized that the fluting of classical Greek columns is a visual remnant from the days when columns were constructed of thin trunks of trees bound together.

Iconostasis : screen-like stand for ikons, usually between the bema and the nave in Orthodox churches.

Olga Broumas was born in Syros, Greece in 1949 and published her first book there in 1967. Moving to the United States, she received her B.A. in architecture from the University of Pennsylvania, and an M.F.A. in creative writing from the University of Oregon. Her first book in English, *Beginning with O,* was selected by Stanley Kunitz for the Yale Younger Poets Award in 1977. She has published two subsequent volumes of poetry, *Soie Sauvage* and *Pastoral Jazz,* and translated two volumes of poetry from the Greek of the Nobel Laureate Odysseas Elytis, *What I Love* and *The Little Mariner* (all from Copper Canyon Press). Her collaboration in the prose poem with Jane Miller, *Black Holes, Black Stockings,* was published by Wesleyan University Press. A recipient of fellowships from the National Endowment for the Arts and the Guggenheim Foundation, she currently lives in Provincetown, Massachusetts, where she is a bodywork therapist. She teaches in the Creative Writing Program at Boston University.

Cover painting is "Night Feather II,"
by Joan Ross Bloedel
(acrylic on canvas, 46½ × 64¾", 1989)

The type is Perpetua, designed by Eric Gill
Type set by The Typeworks, Vancouver, B.C.
Book design by Tree Swenson